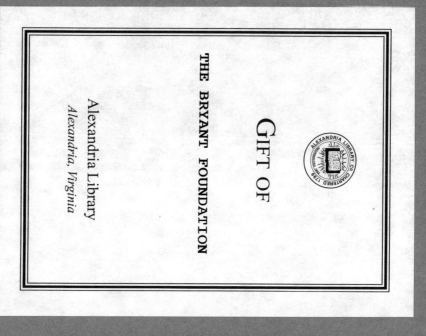

MY BABY

Jeanette Winter

Frances Foster Books
Farrar, Straus and Giroux

NEW YORK

Lettering by Judythe Sieck

Thanks to Adelheid Gealt,
Director of the Indiana University Art Museum,
which sponsored an exhibit and catalogue
of Nakunte Diarra's bògòlan.

Distributed in Canada by Douglas & McIntyre Ltd.
Color separations by Photolitho AG, Gossau-Zürich
Printed and bound in the United States of America by Berryville Graphics
Designed by Jeanette Winter and Judythe Sieck

First edition, 2001

1 3 5 7 9 10 8 6 4 2

Library of Congress Cataloging-in-Publication Data

Winter, Jeanette.
My baby / Jeanette Winter.— 1st ed.
p.   cm.
Summary: As she waits for her baby to be born, a young African woman describes some of
the sights and sounds of her Mali homeland as she creates a beautiful bògòlan cloth for her child.
ISBN 0-374-35103-1
[1. Textile painting—Fiction. 2. Babies—Fiction. 3. Mali—Fiction.] I. Title.
PZ7.W7547 My 2001
[E]—dc21

00-27672

Mali is the home of Nakunte Diarra.
She makes mud-dyed cloth called bɔ̀gɔ̀lan,
carrying on a centuries-old tradition.

"...since God created the world...
bɔ̀gɔ̀lan was here." —N.D.

Whoosh!

The hot wind blows across the savanna to my village.

Whoosh!

The hot wind dries the bògòlan cloth my mama has painted. Her painting stick goes CLICK-CLICK in and out of the mud paint all day long.

Mama gives me a strip of cloth to paint.

"Practice, Nakunte," she says.

I dip my stick in the mud

and begin to paint.

Every day I sit under the arms of the calabash tree, painting my strips. "Good work, Nakunte," Mama says, and gives me a big cloth to paint.

Year after year,
I keep painting the bògòlan.
The whole village comes to me for cloth—

to wear at weddings,

to wrap new babies in,

to wear on the journey to the Promised Land.

My baby will come when the rains come. I must start the bògòlan for my baby.

And when I marry Kuomi, I wear the bògòlan Mama painted just for me.

I search the market
for the whitest cloth.

And when I mix this mud with this leaf, the mud turns black as a starless night.

My baby,
I will paint a bògòlan to wrap you in.
When the rains come,
my baby will come.

The drums scare the little white snake.
Listen, my baby.
to the little white snake as he slithers away.

The leopard's spots hide her.
Listen, my baby,
do you hear
her footsteps
in the bush?

Does iguana know?
He passes by on bent elbows.
Listen, my baby,
to the HISSSS
of his tongue.

Listen, my baby,
do you hear mama crocodile
creeping across the savanna on her short legs?
Will she find the water she is looking for?

Shhh.

I hear a RUSTLE, RUSTLE,
but I see nothing.

My baby,
do you hear the RUSTLE, RUSTLE?

Oh, there, I see chameleon's tail.

He hides from us.

Mmmmmmmm,
the calabash flower
smells so sweet.
Can you smell the
sweetness,
my baby?

Listen, my baby,
to the coo coo coo of the turtledove.
She leaves her footprints in the dust,
one after the other,
until—*whoosh!*—
up she flies—

—up to the little stars that sparkle in the sky.
Soon, my baby, you will see
little stars shining down on you.

There, my baby, the bògòlan is done.

Whoosh!

The hot wind blows it dry.

Oh, the rains are here, my baby. It is time for you to come.

Welcome